INTRODUCING...

Girl

Philip
Gregg

William
Gregg

Mr and Mrs
Gregg

Books by Roald Dahl

THE ENORMOUS CROCODILE
ESIO TROT
FANTASTIC MR FOX
THE GIRAFFE AND THE PELLY AND ME
THE MAGIC FINGER
THE TWITS

For older readers

THE BFG
BOY: TALES OF CHILDHOOD
BOY *and* GOING SOLO
CHARLIE AND THE CHOCOLATE FACTORY
CHARLIE AND THE GREAT GLASS ELEVATOR
THE COMPLETE ADVENTURES OF CHARLIE AND MR WILLY WONKA
DANNY THE CHAMPION OF THE WORLD
GEORGE'S MARVELLOUS MEDICINE
GOING SOLO
JAMES AND THE GIANT PEACH
MATILDA
THE WITCHES

Picture books

DIRTY BEASTS *(with Quentin Blake)*
THE ENORMOUS CROCODILE *(with Quentin Blake)*
THE GIRAFFE AND THE PELLY AND ME *(with Quentin Blake)*
THE MINPINS *(with Patrick Benson)*
REVOLTING RHYMES *(with Quentin Blake)*

Plays

THE BFG: PLAYS FOR CHILDREN *(Adapted by David Wood)*
CHARLIE AND THE CHOCOLATE FACTORY: A PLAY *(Adapted by Richard George)*
FANTASTIC MR FOX: A PLAY *(Adapted by Sally Reid)*
JAMES AND THE GIANT PEACH: A PLAY *(Adapted by Richard George)*
THE TWITS: PLAYS FOR CHILDREN *(Adapted by David Wood)*
THE WITCHES: PLAYS FOR CHILDREN *(Adapted by David Wood)*

Teenage fiction

THE GREAT AUTOMATIC GRAMMATIZATOR AND OTHER STORIES
RHYME STEW
SKIN AND OTHER STORIES
THE VICAR OF NIBBLESWICKE
THE WONDERFUL STORY OF HENRY SUGAR AND SIX MORE

Roald Dahl

The Magic Finger

illustrated by
Quentin Blake

PUFFIN

Find out more about Roald Dahl
by visiting the website at
roalddahl.com

PUFFIN BOOKS

Published by the Penguin Group
Penguin Books Ltd, 80 Strand, London WC2R ORL, England
Penguin Group (USA) Inc., 375 Hudson Street, New York, New York 10014, USA
Penguin Group (Canada), 90 Eglinton Avenue East, Suite 700, Toronto, Ontario, Canada M4P 2Y3
(a division of Pearson Penguin Canada Inc.)
Penguin Ireland, 25 St Stephen's Green, Dublin 2, Ireland (a division of Penguin Books Ltd)
Penguin Group (Australia), 250 Camberwell Road, Camberwell, Victoria 3124, Australia
(a division of Pearson Australia Group Pty Ltd)
Penguin Books India Pvt Ltd, 11 Community Centre, Panchsheel Park, New Delhi – 110 017, India
Penguin Group (NZ), 67 Apollo Drive, Rosedale, North Shore 0632, New Zealand
(a division of Pearson New Zealand Ltd)
Penguin Books (South Africa) (Pty) Ltd, 24 Sturdee Avenue, Rosebank, Johannesburg 2196, South Africa

Penguin Books Ltd, Registered Offices: 80 Strand, London WC2R ORL, England

puffinbooks.com

First published in the USA 1966
Published in Great Britain by George Allen & Unwin 1968
Published in Puffin Books 1974
Reissued with new illustrations 1995
This edition published 2008

1

Text copyright © Roald Dahl Nominee Ltd, 1966
Illustrations copyright © Quentin Blake, 1995
All rights reserved

The moral right of the author and illustrator has been asserted

Set in Monotype Baskerville
Made and printed in England by Clays Ltd, St Ives plc

British Library Cataloguing in Publication Data
A CIP catalogue record for this book is available from the British Library

ISBN: 978-0-141-32268-1

www.greenpenguin.co.uk

This book is for Ophelia and Lucy

The farm next to ours is owned by Mr and Mrs Gregg. The Greggs have two children, both of them boys. Their names are Philip and William. Sometimes I go over to their farm to play with them.

I am a girl and I am eight years old.

Philip is also eight years old.

William is three years older. He is ten.

What?

Oh, all right, then.

He is eleven.

Last week, something very funny happened to the Gregg family. I am going to tell you about it as best I can.

Now the one thing that Mr Gregg and his two boys loved to do more than anything else was to go hunting. Every Saturday morning they would take their guns and go off into the woods to look for animals and birds to shoot. Even Philip, who was only eight years old, had a gun of his own.

I can't stand hunting. I just can't *stand* it. It doesn't seem right to me that men and boys should kill animals just for the fun they get out of it. So I used to try to stop Philip and William from doing it. Every time I went over to their farm I would do my best to talk them out of it, but they only laughed at me.

I even said something about it once to Mr Gregg, but he just walked on past me as if I weren't there.

Then, one Saturday morning, I saw Philip and William coming out of the woods with their father, and they were carrying a lovely young deer.

This made me so cross that I started shouting at them.

The boys laughed and made faces at me, and Mr Gregg told me to go home and mind my own P's and Q's.

Well, that did it!

I saw red.

And before I was able to stop myself, I did something I never meant to do.

I PUT THE MAGIC FINGER ON THEM ALL!

Oh, dear! Oh, dear! I even put it on Mrs Gregg, who wasn't there. I put it on the whole Gregg family.

For months I had been telling myself that I would never put the Magic Finger upon anyone again – not after what happened to my teacher, old Mrs Winter.

Poor old Mrs Winter.

One day we were in class, and she was teaching us spelling. 'Stand up,' she said to me, 'and spell cat.'

'That's an easy one,' I said. *'K-a-t.'*

'You are a stupid little girl!' Mrs Winter said.

'I am not a stupid little girl!' I cried. 'I am a very nice little girl!'

'Go and stand in the corner,' Mrs Winter said.

Then I got cross, and I saw red, and I put the Magic Finger on Mrs Winter good and strong, and almost at once . . .

Guess what?

Whiskers began growing out of her face! They were long black whiskers, just like the ones you see on a cat, only much bigger. And how fast they grew! Before we had time to think, they were out to her ears!

Of course the whole class started screaming with laughter, and then Mrs Winter said, 'Will you be so kind as to tell me what you find so madly funny, all of you?'

And when she turned around to write something on the blackboard we saw that she had grown a *tail* as well! It was a huge bushy tail!

I cannot begin to tell you what happened after that, but if any of you are wondering whether Mrs Winter is quite all right again now, the answer is No. And she never will be.

The Magic Finger is something I have been able to do all my life.

I can't tell you just *how* I do it, because I don't even know myself.

But it always happens when I get cross, when I see red . . .

Then I get very, very hot all over . . .

Then the tip of the forefinger of my right hand begins to tingle most terribly . . .

And suddenly a sort of flash comes out of me, a quick flash, like something electric.

It jumps out and touches the person who has made me cross . . .

And after that the Magic Finger is upon him or her, and things begin to happen . . .

Well, the Magic Finger was now upon the whole of the Gregg family, and there was no taking it off again.

I ran home and waited for things to happen.

They happened fast.

I shall now tell you what those things were. I got the whole story from Philip and William the next morning, after it was all over.

In the afternoon of the very same day that I put the Magic Finger on the Gregg family, Mr Gregg and Philip and William went out hunting once again. This time they were going after wild ducks, so they headed towards the lake.

In the first hour they got ten birds.

In the next hour they got another six.

'What a day!' cried Mr Gregg. 'This is the best yet!' He was beside himself with joy.

Just then four more wild ducks flew over their heads. They were flying very low. They were easy to hit.

BANG! BANG! BANG! BANG! went the guns.

The ducks flew on.

'We missed!' said Mr Gregg. 'That's funny.'

Then, to everyone's surprise, the four ducks turned around and came flying right back to the guns.

'Hey!' said Mr Gregg. 'What on earth are they doing? They are really asking for it this time!' He shot at them again. So did the boys. And again they all missed!

Mr Gregg got very red in the face. 'It's the light,' he said. 'It's getting too dark to see. Let's go home.'

So they started for home, carrying with them the sixteen birds they had shot before.

But the four ducks would not leave them alone. They now began flying around and around the hunters as they walked away.

Mr Gregg did not like it one bit. 'Be off!' he cried, and he shot at them many more times, but it was no good. He simply could not hit them. All the way home those four ducks flew around in the sky above their heads, and nothing would make them go away.

Late that night, after Philip and William had gone to bed, Mr Gregg went outside to get some wood for the fire.

He was crossing the yard when all at once he heard the call of a wild duck in the sky.

He stopped and looked up. The night was very still. There was a thin yellow moon over the trees on the hill, and the sky was filled with stars. Then Mr Gregg heard the noise of wings flying low over

his head, and he saw the four ducks, dark against the night sky, flying very close together. They were going around and around the house.

Mr Gregg forgot about the firewood, and hurried back indoors. He was now quite afraid. He did not like what was going on. But he said nothing about it to Mrs Gregg. All he said was, 'Come on, let's go to bed. I feel tired.'

So they went to bed and to sleep.

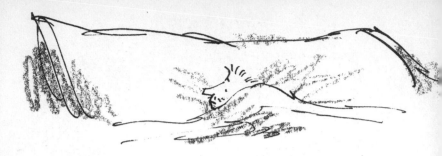

When morning came, Mr Gregg was the first to wake up.

He opened his eyes.

He was about to put out a hand for his watch, to see the time.

But his hand wouldn't come out.

'That's funny,' he said. 'Where is my hand?'

He lay still, wondering what was up.

Maybe he had hurt that hand in some way?

He tried the other hand.

That wouldn't come out either.

He sat up.

Then, for the first time, he saw what he looked like!

He gave a yell and jumped out of bed.

Mrs Gregg woke up. And when she saw Mr Gregg standing there on the floor, *she* gave a yell, too.

For he was now a tiny little man!

He was maybe as tall as the seat of a chair, but no taller.

And where his arms had been, he had a pair of duck's wings instead!

'But . . . but . . . but . . .' cried Mrs Gregg, going purple in the face. 'My dear man, what's happened to you?'

'What's happened to both of us, you mean!' shouted Mr Gregg.

It was Mrs Gregg's turn now to jump out of bed.

She ran to look at herself in the glass. But she was not tall enough to see into it. She was even smaller than Mr Gregg, and she, too, had got wings instead of arms.

'Oh! Oh! Oh! Oh!' sobbed Mrs Gregg.

'This is witches' work!' cried Mr Gregg. And both of them started running around the room, flapping their wings.

A minute later Philip and William burst in. The same thing had happened to them. They had wings and no arms. And they were *really* tiny. They were about as big as robins.

'Mama! Mama! Mama!' chirruped Philip. 'Look, Mama, we can fly!' And they flew up into the air.

'Come down at once!' said Mrs Gregg. 'You're much too high!' But before she could say another word, Philip and William had flown right out the window.

Mr and Mrs Gregg ran to the window and looked out. The two tiny boys were now high up in the sky.

Then Mrs Gregg said to Mr Gregg, 'Do you think *we* could do that, my dear?'

'I don't see why not,' Mr Gregg said. 'Come on, let's try.'

Mr Gregg began to flap his wings hard, and all at once, up he went.

Then Mrs Gregg did the same.

'Help!' she cried as she started going up. 'Save me!'

'Come on,' said Mr Gregg. 'Don't be afraid.'

So out the window they flew, far up into the sky, and it did not take them long to catch up with Philip and William.

Soon the whole family was flying around and around together.

'Oh, isn't it lovely!' cried William. 'I've always wanted to know what it feels like to be a bird!'

'Your wings are not getting tired, are they, dear?' Mr Gregg asked Mrs Gregg.

'Not at all,' Mrs Gregg said. 'I could go on for ever!'

'Hey, look down there!' said Philip. 'Somebody is walking in our garden!'

They all looked down, and there below them, in their own garden, they saw four *enormous* wild ducks! The ducks were as big as men, and what is more, they had great long arms, like men, instead of wings.

The ducks were walking in a line to the door of the Greggs' house, swinging their arms and holding their beaks high in the air.

'Stop!' called the tiny Mr Gregg, flying down low over their heads. 'Go away! That's my house!'

The ducks looked up and quacked. The first one put out a hand and opened the door of the house and went in. The others went in after him. The door shut.

The Greggs flew down and sat on the wall near the door. Mrs Gregg began to cry.

'Oh, dear! Oh, dear!' she sobbed. 'They have taken our house. What *shall* we do? We have no place to go!'

Even the boys began to cry a bit now.

'We will be eaten by cats and foxes in the night!' said Philip.

'I want to sleep in my own bed!' said William.

'Now then,' said Mr Gregg. 'It isn't any good crying. That won't help us. Shall I tell you what we are going to do?'

'What?' they said.

Mr Gregg looked at them and smiled. 'We are going to build a nest.'

'A nest!' they said. 'Can we do that?'

'We *must* do it,' said Mr Gregg. 'We've got to have somewhere to sleep. Follow me.'

They flew off to a tall tree, and right at the top of it Mr Gregg chose the place for the nest.

'Now we want sticks,' he said. 'Lots and lots of little sticks. Off you go, all of you, and find them and bring them back here.'

'But we have no hands!' said Philip.

'Then use your mouths.'

Mrs Gregg and the children flew off. Soon they were back, carrying sticks in their mouths.

Mr Gregg took the sticks and started to build the nest.

'More,' he said. 'I want more and more and more sticks. Keep going.'

The nest began to grow. Mr Gregg was very good at making the sticks stick together.

After a while he said, 'That's enough sticks. Now I want leaves and feathers and things like that to make the inside nice and soft.'

The building of the nest went on and on. It took a long time. But at last it was finished.

'Try it,' said Mr Gregg, hopping back. He was very pleased with his work.

'Oh, isn't it lovely!' cried Mrs Gregg, going into it and sitting down. 'I feel I might lay an egg any moment!'

The others all got in beside her.

'How warm it is!' said William.

'And what fun to be living so high up,' said Philip. 'We may be small, but nobody can hurt us up here.'

'But what about food?' said Mrs Gregg. 'We haven't had a thing to eat all day.'

'That's right,' Mr Gregg said. 'So we will now fly back to the house and go in by an open window and get the tin of biscuits when the ducks aren't looking.'

'Oh, we will be pecked to bits by those dirty great ducks!' cried Mrs Gregg.

'We shall be very careful, my love,' said Mr Gregg. And off they went.

But when they got to the house, they found all the windows and doors closed. There was no way in.

'Just look at that beastly duck cooking at my stove!' cried Mrs Gregg as she flew past the kitchen window. 'How dare she!'

'And look at *that* one holding my lovely gun!' shouted Mr Gregg.

'One of them is lying in my bed!' yelled William, looking into a top window.

'And one of them is playing with my electric train!' cried Philip.

'Oh, dear! Oh, dear!' said Mrs Gregg. 'They have taken over our whole house! We shall never get it back. And what *are* we going to eat?'

'I will *not* eat worms,' said Philip. 'I would rather die.'

'Or slugs,' said William.

Mrs Gregg took the two boys under her wings and hugged them. 'Don't worry,' she said. 'I can mince it all up very fine and you won't even know the difference. Lovely slugburgers. Delicious wormburgers.'

'Oh no!' cried William.

'Never!' said Philip.

'Disgusting!' said Mr Gregg. 'Just because we have wings, we don't have to eat bird food. We shall eat apples instead. Our trees are full of them. Come on!'

So they flew off to an apple tree.

But to eat an apple without holding it in your hands is not at all easy. Every time you try to get your teeth into it, it just pushes away. In the end, they were able to get a few small bites each. And then it began to get dark, so they all flew back to the nest and lay down to sleep.

It must have been at about this time that I, back in my own house, picked up the telephone and tried to call Philip. I wanted to see if the family was all right.

'Hello,' I said.

'Quack!' said a voice at the other end.

'Who is it?' I asked.

'Quack-quack!'

'Philip,' I said, 'is that you?'

'Quack-quack-quack-quack-quack!'

'Oh, stop it!' I said.

Then there came a very funny noise. It was like a bird laughing.

I put down the telephone quickly.

'Oh, that Magic Finger!' I cried. 'What *has* it done to my friends?'

That night, while Mr and Mrs Gregg and Philip and William were trying to get some sleep up in the high nest, a great wind began to blow. The tree rocked from side to side, and everyone, even Mr

Gregg, was afraid that the nest would fall down.
Then came the rain. It rained and rained, and the
water ran into the nest and they all got as wet as
could be – and oh, it was a bad, bad night!

At last the morning came, and with it the warm sun.

'Well!' said Mrs Gregg. 'Thank goodness that's over! I never want to sleep in a nest again!' She got up and looked over the side . . .

'Help!' she cried. 'Look! Look down there!'

'What is it, my love?' said Mr Gregg. He stood up and peeped over the side.

He got the surprise of his life!

On the ground below them stood the four enormous ducks, as tall as men, and three of them were holding guns in their hands. One had Mr Gregg's gun, one had Philip's gun, and one had William's gun.

The guns were all pointing right up at the nest.

'No! No! No!' called out Mr and Mrs Gregg, both together. 'Don't shoot! Please don't shoot!'

'Why not?' said one of the ducks. It was the one who wasn't holding a gun. 'You are always shooting at *us*.'

'Oh, but that's not the same!' said Mr Gregg. 'We are *allowed* to shoot ducks!'

'Who allows you?' asked the duck.

'We allow each other,' said Mr Gregg.

'Very nice,' said the duck. 'And now *we* are going to allow each other to shoot you.'

(I would have loved to have seen Mr Gregg's face just then.)

'Oh, *please*!' cried Mrs Gregg. 'My two little children are up here with us! You wouldn't shoot my *children*!'

'Yesterday you shot *my* children,' said the duck. 'You shot all six of my children.'

'I'll never do it again!' cried Mr Gregg. 'Never, never, never!'

'Do you really mean that?' asked the duck.

'I *do* mean it!' said Mr Gregg. 'I'll never shoot another duck as long as I live!'

'That is not good enough,' said the duck. 'What about deer?'

'I'll do anything you say if you will only put down those guns!' cried Mr Gregg. 'I'll never shoot another duck or another deer or anything else again!'

'Will you give me your word on that?' said the duck.

'I will! I will!' said Mr Gregg.

'Will you throw away your guns?' asked the duck.

'I will break them into tiny bits!' said Mr Gregg. 'And never again need you be afraid of me or my family.'

'Very well,' said the duck. 'You may now come down. And by the way, may I congratulate you on the nest. For a first effort it's pretty good.'

Mr and Mrs Gregg and Philip and William hopped out of the nest and flew down.

Then all at once everything went black before
their eyes, and they couldn't see. At the same time

a funny feeling came over them all, and they heard
a great wind blowing in their ears.

Then the black that was before their eyes turned
to blue, to green, to red, and then to gold, and
suddenly, there they were, standing in lovely bright

sunshine in their own garden, near their own house, and everything was back to normal once again.

'Our wings have gone!' cried Mr Gregg. 'And our arms have come back!'

'And we are not tiny any more!' laughed Mrs Gregg. 'Oh, I am so glad!'

Philip and William began dancing about with joy.

Then, high above their heads, they heard the call of a wild duck. They all looked up, and they saw the four birds, lovely against the blue sky, flying very close together, heading back to the lake in the woods.

It must have been about half an hour later that I myself walked into the Greggs' garden. I had come to see how things were going, and I must admit I was expecting the worst. At the gate I stopped and stared. It was a queer sight.

In one corner Mr Gregg was smashing all three guns into tiny pieces with a huge hammer.

In another corner Mrs Gregg was placing beautiful flowers upon sixteen tiny mounds of soil which I learned later were the graves of the ducks that had been shot the day before.

And in the middle of the yard stood Philip and William, with a sack of their father's best barley beside them. They were surrounded by ducks, doves, pigeons, sparrows, robins, larks, and many other kinds that I did not know, and the birds were eating the barley that the boys were scattering by the handful.

'Good morning, Mr Gregg,' I said.

Mr Gregg lowered his hammer and looked at me. 'My name is not Gregg any more,' he said. 'In honour of my feathered friends, I have changed it from Gregg to Egg.'

'And I am Mrs Egg,' said Mrs Gregg.

'What happened?' I asked. They seemed to have gone completely dotty, all four of them.

Philip and William then began to tell me the whole story. When they had finished, William said, 'Look! There's the nest! Can you see it? Right up in the top of the tree! That's where we slept last night!'

'I built it *all* myself,' Mr Egg said proudly. 'Every stick of it.'

'If you don't believe us,' Mrs Egg said, 'just go into the house and take a look at the bathroom. It's a mess.'

'They filled the tub right up to the brim,' Philip said. 'They must have been swimming around in it all night! And feathers everywhere!'

'Ducks like water,' Mr Egg said. 'I'm glad they had a good time.'

Just then, from somewhere over by the lake, there came a loud BANG!

'Someone's shooting!' I cried.

'That'll be Jim Cooper,' Mr Egg said. 'Him and his three boys. They're shooting mad, those Coopers are, the whole family.'

Suddenly I started to see red . . .

Then I got very hot all over . . .

Then the tip of my finger began tingling most terribly. I could feel the power building up and up inside me . . .

I turned and started running towards the lake as fast as I could.

'Hey!' shouted Mr Egg. 'What's up? Where are you going?'

'To find the Coopers,' I called back.

'But why?'

'You wait and see!' I said. 'They'll be nesting in the trees tonight, every one of them!'

ROALD DAHL

'I think probably kindness is my number one attribute in a human being. I'll put it before any of the things like courage or bravery or generosity or anything else. If you're kind, that's it.'

'I am totally convinced that most grown-ups have completely forgotten what it is like to be a child between the ages of five and ten . . . I can remember exactly what it was like. I am certain I can.'

'When I first thought about writing the book *Charlie and the Chocolate Factory*, I never originally meant to have children in it at all!'

'If I had my way, I would remove January from the calendar altogether and have an extra July instead.'

'You can write about anything for children as long as you've got humour.'

SAYS

Roald Dahl's
FAVOURITE THINGS

There was a table in the writing hut on which Roald Dahl kept
his collection of special things. And they're all still there.

spine shavings

silver
wrapper ball

Hurricane
model
plane

rock
containing
opal

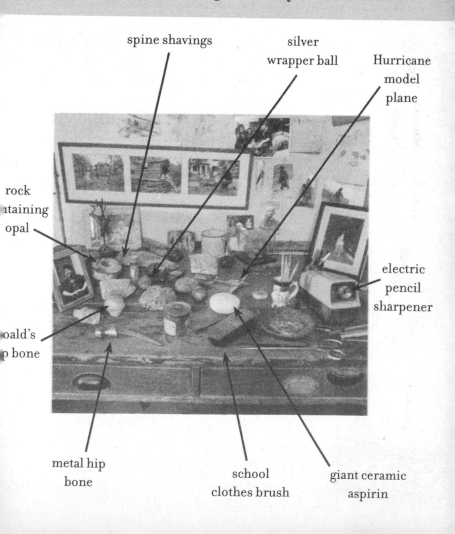

electric
pencil
sharpener

Roald's
hip bone

metal hip
bone

school
clothes brush

giant ceramic
aspirin

R
O
A
L
D
D
A
H
L

1916 Roald Dahl was born on 13 September in Llandaff in Wales.

1925 Roald was sent to boarding school – St Peter's School in Weston-super-Mare.

1929 Roald went to Repton, another boarding school. It was here that he helped to test new chocolate bars for Cadbury's. Favourites included Aero, Crunchie, KitKat, Mars and Smarties.

1934 Roald Dahl left school and went to work for Shell, the big oil company, because he wanted to travel to magical faraway places like Africa and China.

1936 Shell sent him to east Africa. He hated the snakes!

1939 Roald Dahl joined the RAF at the start of the Second World War. He became a fighter pilot, flying Hurricane aeroplanes across the Mediterranean Sea.

1940 His plane crashed in the Western Desert, in north Africa, and he received severe injuries to his head, nose and back.

1942 Roald was sent to the USA to work in the British Embassy (and some say he was also a spy!). His first adult story was published and he wrote his first story for children, about mischievous creatures called Gremlins. Walt Disney started work on turning it into a film and Roald went to Hollywood.

1943 Movie plans ground to a halt, but *The Gremlins* was published in the USA, Britain and Australia. It was Roald's first book.

 1953 Roald's book of spine-tingling stories for adults, *Someone Like You*, was published and was a huge success in the USA.

 1961 *James and the Giant Peach* was published in the USA, followed by *Charlie and the Chocolate Factory* in 1964. It was an instant hit with children.

 1967 *James* and *Charlie* were finally published in Britain and have become two of the most successful and popular children's books ever.

 1971 The first *Charlie* film was made as *Willy Wonka and the Chocolate Factory*. Other films followed: *The BFG* and *Danny the Champion of the World* in 1989; *The Witches* in 1990; *James and the Giant Peach* and *Matilda* in 1996; the second *Charlie and the Chocolate Factory*, starring Johnny Depp, came out in 2005.

 1978 Roald Dahl's partnership with Quentin Blake began with the publication of *The Enormous Crocodile*.

 1990 Roald Dahl died on 23 November, aged seventy-four.

2006 and beyond Roald Dahl Day is celebrated all over the world on 13 September to mark Roald Dahl's birthday. Visit **roalddahlday.info** to join the fun.

Roald Dahl's

Roald Dahl's father, Harald, was Norwegian. When he was fourteen he had a terrible accident and had to have his left arm amputated – but, in spite of missing a hand, he always managed to tie his own shoelaces. Harald Dahl moved to Cardiff when he was a young man and started a very successful shipbroking business.

Roald's mother, Sofie, was also Norwegian. She married Harald in 1911 and they had five children: Astri, Alfhild, Roald, Else and Asta. Roald was the only boy in a family of sisters.

FROM LEFT TO RIGHT: Asta, Else, Alfhild, Roald

Sadly, Astri died from appendicitis when she was seven, and Roald's father died of a broken heart two months later. Roald was only three at the time, so he never really knew his father.

Roald Dahl also had a much older half-brother and half-sister, Louis and Ellen, as his father had been married before. They all went on holiday together to Norway every summer: Roald's mother and the six children.

Roald was very close to his sisters, particularly his big sister, Alfhild or Alf. His middle sister, Else, hated school (like Roald). When her mother sent her to boarding school in Switzerland, Else ate her train ticket so that she would have to be collected and brought home. Asta, Roald's youngest sister, joined the RAF during the Second World War. She flew in barrage balloons in the UK and later received a medal from the King of Norway.

Roald Dahl himself had five children: Olivia, Tessa, Theo, Ophelia and Lucy. Tragically, Olivia died of measles when she was seven — the same age as his eldest sister when she died.

Roald Dahl's
SCHOOL REPORTS

In 1929, when he was thirteen, Roald Dahl was sent to boarding school. You would expect him to get wonderful marks in English – but his school reports were *not* good!

My end-of-term reports from this school are of some interest. Here are just four of them, copied word for word from the original documents:

SUMMER TERM, 1930 (aged 14).
English Composition.

"I have never met a boy who so persistently writes the exact opposite of what he means. He seems incapable of marshalling his thoughts on paper."

EASTER TERM, 1931 (aged 15). *English Composition.*
"A persistent muddler. Vocabulary negligible, sentences malconstructed. He reminds me of a camel."

SUMMER TERM, 1932 (aged 16). *English Composition.*
"This boy is an indolent and illiterate member of the class."

AUTUMN TERM, 1932 (aged 17). *English Composition.*
"Consistently idle. Ideas limited."

Little wonder that it never entered my head to become a writer in those days.

Find out more about Roald Dahl at school in *Boy*.

WEIRD AND WONDERFUL FACTS ABOUT
Roald Dahl

He was very tall — six feet five and three-quarter inches, or nearly two metres. His nickname in the RAF was Lofty, while Walt Disney called him Stalky (because he was like a beanstalk!).

His nickname at home was the Apple, because he was the apple of his mother's eye (which means her favourite!).

He pretended to have appendicitis when he was nine because he was so homesick in his first two weeks at boarding school. He fooled the matron and the school doctor and was sent home. But he couldn't fool his own doctor, who made him promise never to do it again.

He was a terrible speller, but he liked playing Scrabble.

He didn't like cats — but he did like dogs, birds and goats.

Roald Dahl wrote the screenplay for the James Bond film *You Only Live Twice*.

He once had a tame magpie.

He was a keen photographer at school and, when he was eighteen, won two prizes: one from the Royal Photographic Society in London and another from the Photographic Society of Holland.

A DAY IN THE LIFE OF
Roald Dahl

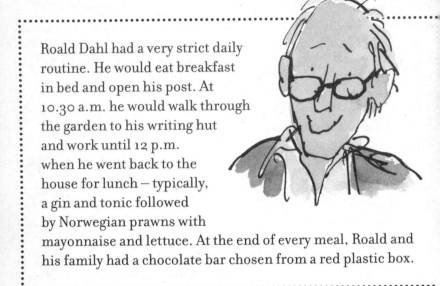

Roald Dahl had a very strict daily routine. He would eat breakfast in bed and open his post. At 10.30 a.m. he would walk through the garden to his writing hut and work until 12 p.m. when he went back to the house for lunch – typically, a gin and tonic followed by Norwegian prawns with mayonnaise and lettuce. At the end of every meal, Roald and his family had a chocolate bar chosen from a red plastic box.

After a snooze, he would take a flask of tea back to the writing hut and work from 4 p.m. till 6 p.m. He would be back at the house at exactly six o'clock, ready for his dinner.

He always wrote in pencil and only ever used a very particular kind of yellow pencil with a rubber on the end. Before he started writing, Roald made sure he had six sharpened pencils in a jar by his side. They lasted for two hours before needing to be resharpened.

Roald was *very* particular about the kind of paper he used as well. He wrote all of his books on American yellow legal pads, which were sent to him from New York. He wrote and rewrote until he was sure that every word was just right. A lot of yellow paper was thrown away. Once a month, when his large wastepaper basket was full to overflowing, he made a bonfire just outside his writing hut (where one of the white walls was soon streaked with black soot).

Once Roald had finished writing a book, he gave the pile of yellow scribbled paper to Wendy, his secretary, and she turned it into a neat printed manuscript to send to his publisher.

Roald Dahl's
ADVENTURES

When Roald was sixteen, he decided to go off on his own to holiday in France. He crossed the Channel from Dover to Calais with £24 in his pocket (a lot of money in 1933). Roald wanted to see the Mediterranean Sea, so he took the train first to Paris, then on to Marseilles where he got on a bus that went all the way along the coastal road towards Monte Carlo. He finished up at a place called St Jean Cap Ferrat and stayed there for ten days, wandering around by himself and doing whatever he wanted. It was his first taste of absolute freedom – and what it was like to be a grown-up.

He travelled back home the same way but, by the time he reached Dover, he had absolutely no money left. Luckily a fellow passenger gave him ten shillings (50p in today's money!) for his tram fare home. Roald never forgot this kindness and generosity.

When Roald was seventeen he signed up to go to Newfoundland, Canada, with 'The Public Schools' Exploring Society'. Together with thirty other boys, he spent three weeks trudging over a desolate landscape with an enormous rucksack. It weighed so much that he needed someone to help him hoist it on to his back every morning. The boys lived on pemmican (strips of pressed meat, fat, and berries) and lentils, and they experimented with eating boiled lichen and reindeer moss because they were so hungry. It was a genuine adventure and left Roald fit and ready for anything!

'The finest illustrator of children's books in the world today!' – Roald Dahl

Roald Dahl and Quentin Blake make a perfect partnership of words and illustrations, but when Roald started writing, he had many different illustrators. Quentin started working with him in 1976 (the first book he illustrated was *The Enormous Crocodile*, published in 1978) and from then on they worked together until Roald's death. Quentin ended up illustrating all of Roald Dahl's books, with the exception of *The Minpins*.

To begin with, Quentin was a bit nervous about working with such a very famous author, but by the time they collaborated on *The BFG*, they had become firm friends. Quentin never knew anything about a new story until the manuscript arrived. 'You'll have some fun with this,' Roald would say – or, 'You'll have some trouble with this.' Quentin would make lots of rough drawings to take along to Gipsy House, where he would show them to Roald and see what he thought. Roald Dahl liked his books to be packed with illustrations – Quentin ended up drawing twice as many pictures for *The BFG* as he had originally been asked for.

Quentin Blake's favourite Roald Dahl book is *The BFG*. When he wasn't quite sure what the BFG's footwear would look like, Roald actually sent one of his old sandals through the post to Quentin – and that's what he drew!

Quentin Blake was born on 16 December 1932. His first drawing was published when he was sixteen, and he has written and illustrated many of his own books, as well as Roald Dahl's. Besides being an illustrator he taught for over twenty years at the Royal College of Art – he is a real professor! In 1999 Quentin Blake was chosen to be the first Children's Laureate. In 2005 he was awarded the CBE for services to children's literature.

Find out more at quentinblake.com

GOBBLEFUNK

Roald Dahl loved playing around with words and inventing new ones. In *The BFG* he gave this strange language an even stranger name – Gobblefunk!

BAGGLEPIPES

Bagpipes: famous Scottish wind instrument.

BOGGLEBOX

A school for young children (generally boys).

CRABCRUNCHER

Crabcrunchers live high up on cliffs by the sea. They're very rare.

FROTHBUNGLING

Means stupid.

GLORIUMPTIOUS

Gloriously wonderful.

HUMAN BEAN

This is the name the giants in *The BFG* give to human beings.

JUMPSQUIFFLING

Something absolutely huge.

LIXIVATE

Very gruesome! You are squashed and turned to liquid at the same time.

MUGGLED

To be muggled means to be a bit confused.

QUOGWINKLE

A quogwinkle is an alien from outer space.

SNITCHING

Stealing and thieving.

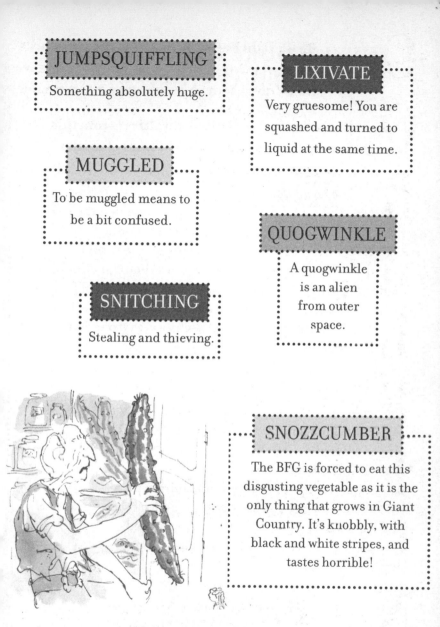

SNOZZCUMBER

The BFG is forced to eat this disgusting vegetable as it is the only thing that grows in Giant Country. It's knobbly, with black and white stripes, and tastes horrible!

TROGGLEHUMPER

The worst kind of dream: a nightmare.

THERE'S MORE TO ROALD DAHL THAN GREAT STORIES . . .

Did you know that 10% of author royalties* from this book go to help the work of the Roald Dahl charities?

The Roald Dahl Foundation supports specialist paediatric Roald Dahl nurses throughout the UK caring for children with epilepsy, blood disorders and acquired brain injury. It also provides practical help for children and young people with brain, blood and literacy problems – all causes close to Roald Dahl during his lifetime – through grants to UK hospitals and charities as well as to individual children and their families.

The Roald Dahl Museum and Story Centre, based in Great Missenden just outside London, is in the Buckinghamshire village where Roald Dahl lived and wrote. At the heart of the Museum, created to inspire a love of reading and writing, is his unique archive of letters and manuscripts. As well as two fun-packed biographical galleries, the Museum boasts an interactive Story Centre. It is a place for the family, teachers and their pupils to explore the exciting world of creativity and literacy.

The Roald Dahl Foundation is a registered charity no. 1004230

The Roald Dahl Museum and Story Centre is a registered charity no. 1085853

The Roald Dahl Charitable Trust, a newly established charity, supports the work of RDF and RDMSC

* Donated royalties are net of commission

roalddahlfoundation.org
roalddahlmuseum.org